SIMON
SAYS

For Mej —
Here's to poetry
& health & joy!
love,

10.27.00

ALSO BY THE AUTHOR

Hyena
Autumn Sequence (chapbook)

SIMON

SAYS

JAN FREEMAN

PARIS
PRESS

Ashfield, Massachusetts

Paris Press extends heartfelt thanks to the Massachusetts Cultural Council, the Sonia
Raiziss Giop Charitable Trust, the Art Angels Fund at the Community Foundation of
Western Massachusetts, and to the individuals whose generosity made the publication of
Simon Says possible. We are indebted to the support of Sally Montgomery and
Anne Goldstein, to the hard work and dedication of Lydia Peterson and Jenna Evans,
and to the generosity of Ann R. Stokes.

Painting on the cover is "Letter Ghost" (1937) by Paul Klee.
Colored paste (mixture of pigment, chalk, and starch) on newspaper, $13 \times 19\frac{1}{4}''$.
The Museum of Modern Art, New York. Purchase.
Photograph © 2000 The Museum of Modern Art, New York.

This book is a creative act. Any resemblance to persons living or dead
or to actual incidents or events is purely coincidental.

Library of Congress Cataloging-in-Publication Data
Freeman, Jan.
Simon says / by Jan Freeman. — 1st ed,
p.   cm.
ISBN 0-9638183-4-1 (alk.paper)
I. Title.

PS3556.R389 S5   2000
811'.54 — dc21   00-057993

First Edition.

0 9 8 7 6 5 4 3 2 1

Printed in the United States of America

ACKNOWLEDGMENTS

Many thanks to the editors and publishers of the following journals, in which some of the poems in this volume previously appeared: *The American Poetry Review, The American Voice, Chelsea, The Drunken Boat, The Marlboro Review, The Massachusetts Review,* and *The North Atlantic Review.*

I offer gratitude to my friends in poetry, Theo Oktenberg, Siena Sanderson, Tsipi Keller, Robin Becker, Tzivia Gover, and Fred Smock for their feedback about many of the poems in this book. Thanks to Carlotta Crissey for a place of beauty and comfort in all seasons, to Nick and Elspeth Macdonald for peace on Slough Pond, to Ann R. Stokes for a respite in the Studio on Welcome Hill Road, and to the late Henry Sauerwein and the Helene Wurlitzer Foundation of New Mexico, where this collection of poems began. Many thanks also to Jody Stewart for poetry mornings at Elmer's. And to Mary Lucas for friendship.

A skyful of gratitude to Ivan Holmes and Judythe Sieck for transforming *Simon Says* into a beautiful breathing book.

Immeasurable thanks to Ellie Lazarus and to Lyndy Pye for restoration of the spirit and the heart.

For E.D., T.O.,
R.S., and L.C.F.

CONTENTS

SECTION ONE

Tenderness Killed the Cat   3

If Tired Meant Heart   5

A Winter's Story   6

Simon Says   8

Happiness Killed the Cat   10

Missing Brassiere   12

As If Her Breath   14

Kiss   15

Will Killed the Cat   16

On the Subject of Suicide   18

Contra Dance   21

Her Long Spine   23

SECTION TWO

Comfort Killed the Cat   29

October Poems   31

Miss Mary Mack Mack Mack, Another Version   38

Are You My Cake to Eat and Love?   42

Cat's Dream: Praise Killed the Cat   45

That Day   46

A Horse   49

Tin   52

Stupidity Killed the Cat   54

A Likely Story   56

Morning Mantra   64

Some Things Continue When You're Dead   66

SECTION THREE

Greed Killed the Cat   71

Rain   74

Money   78

Leaves   79

Grandiosity Killed the Cat   81

My Country 'Tis of Thee   83

When Fear Was Small   88

Doe See Doe!   89

Alchemy   95

The Cat Alive   98

SIMON
SAYS

SECTION
ONE

TENDERNESS KILLED THE CAT

It started with an old train
leaves as tears
broken bones
Then the cat walked by as a baseball bat
swung over the path
Some friends are found through enemies
a story old but true
Choose a hatred find a soul
whose hatred burns alive like yours
Friends for the duration then
if hatred lasts
The cat walked by and I walked by
the baseball bat swung round and back
and we examined bat's full face
to see the *punim* friendship fed
It was a woman then a man
alike but not in friendship's realm
Cat ran fast and I ran fast
and baseball bat came down and down
"I need the hatred hatred frees
and so do broken bones
and so do lies or poison"
said the cat
"all cruelty
keeps me intact"
I stroked and I stroked and I
stroked the cat
till she fell into a deep deep sleep

and I kissed the cat
on the tip of her ear
Then twitch went her bones
and snap went her head
and asleep with love and innocence
the cat was dead.

IF TIRED MEANT HEART

If tired meant heart or rage my own day
my toughness all mask or leaf on the ground
when skies are bright red or hilltops not black
faggot a fire, the queer my last stone
a pocket or shot, a family truce, and you all lit up
all merit or cradle there to hold tightly to any bright anthem
swelling a love song, all trust like a soldier
If I were blue shadow and you a green pillow
if I were a hunter and you a green tree
if my head not fire but water, entirely
open for anger or terror or pain
When losses are strangers and strangers desire
garments as ambush or skin energy
then eyes steeped in luster might blind that quick ambush
and capture the marshal who swings for the jester
who tosses her bells unprepared for the mire
that fastens its skin as the cage splits apart
and there for the world to see
true love's great entity
bells between ribs and ribbons in knots —
that curve as my love once curved outward
to touch some heat, faceless
you turn from me, hands on my shoulders —
nothing but fingers and shapely carved stones
Remember your home, you sing, casket or cradle sing
Once I was lively, my mind was my body
heart was an organ, still, muscle not emblem then
tenderness simply touch rather than world to me.

A WINTER'S STORY

Once a bear found a yellow window
and she sat beside the window during the day
She watched the dogs eat breakfast and clean their paws
She watched a lady wash dishes and eat a piece of bread covered with jam
Once a bear slept through winter and dreamed of a yellow window
No one woke the bear
Snow covered her den
Night and day were the same for the bear
Once a woman lit a fire
and imagined that the flames were cities
people ran from door to door leaving gifts and love letters
Sometimes they ate bread and jam and watched the fire
Once two dogs slept during the day and cleaned their paws
at the same time in the late morning and early evening
They ate spaghetti for special occasions
and slept side by side
Once the sky was the sky
and no one spoke to the meadow
The maples waved through loneliness
The hilltop was a flag signaling seasons changing
Some birds slept in the maples some slept in the birch
Some were loyal some were fickle
Once an orange fish noticed a bear admiring herself in the pond's reflection
Once a bear grabbed an orange fish under water
She stuffed it in her mouth
Better than jam and bread, she said
The dogs saw the bear and ran to the hilltop
The lady watched the dogs run and followed them with a long gun

The maples and birch swayed happily

The dogs and the lady stood beside them

and watched the bear swallow the orange fish

No one thought about the yellow window

They all ran around outside

and then the snow fell like feathers onto the ground.

SIMON SAYS

I was hated as a child.
Simon says, Blow your nose.
My father worked, my mother froze
and I was one day meant to be
an entity of their desires
and hidden when their love expired.

Simon says, Dance fast dance slow
to any simple melody.
Simon says, The past is there —
behind your shadow, like a tree.

Simon says, If you love fire
light a match and burn like wood,
but know that fire will not replace
the heat that is elusive still,
which mother might have wrapped and stitched
through and through your growing soul,
and father might have left you with
before his world uncurled like yarn.

Simon says, Day begins
with nighttime folded in its veins.
Simon says, Sing a while
that Russian love song, Grandpa's smile.

Simon says, when hatred grows
around your neck through childhood,

kind words and then a gentle face
become two mirrors of disgrace,
and even one soft voice may dwell
against your will to save yourself;
because a child who knows best hate
has only solitude for fate.

Simon says, Scratch an itch.
Simon says, Butter the bread.
Simon says, Live while you can —
It's so much harder when you're dead.

HAPPINESS KILLED THE CAT

The cat woke up and growled and said
"I like it better when I'm dead"
She kicked the milk bowl by her bed
then howled and hid, then scratched and fled
Two days later the cat felt better
"It's true the dark can get to you —
it's worse than broken bones or flu"
said the cat as she arched in a spot of sun
She leapt on a tabletop, perched on a windowsill
the world was a bright light, the world was a flower bed
"I like the way this fits"
she said and licked her fur and chewed an itch
Then up she sprang on her clean paws
she twirled true joy then mewed delight
around she pranced free of her plight —
that winter cave, the sorrow tight around her neck
where dread began
"Oh happy oh happy oh happy I am"
she purred as the night in the trees began
Without a glance behind or up
she sprang and stalked
as if spring tucked her tail
under her breath
Then tiptoe here and tiptoe near the stream
the woods a patch of weeds
a fox sprang fast with eyes all greed
and whiskers, points and legs all speed
and the cat mid-leap remembered sleep —

Shadows were a deep hole, sky was a pinhole

"Meow," she moaned between sharp teeth

"I once was angry and then I was happy and happier and happier and happier I sang—

everything was beautiful the dirt was even beautiful

I wiggled as I stretched and twirled as I ran"

Then she waved to the pine trees, pictured her old milk bowl

blew kisses to the green grass

"Happiness was here and happiness was good, but now"

said the cat, "I'm not happy to be food"

Down came the fox teeth, swirl went the fox tongue

"Once lonely," grinned the fox, full, "now you're among!"

"I always wanted happiness"

the cat said, somber

"But what's the use of a happy past

when you've got no more tomorrow?"

MISSING BRASSIERE

It might be with the tablecloths
or under the bed or in the sheets
or on the chair beneath the other
discarded clothes of passion
It might be by the shower door
the closet door the bedroom door
or out by the roses or under the peach tree
next to the cucumbers —
after the party, unclasped and thrown
against some heap
after the guests had gone to sleep
tucked in their distant beds by three in the morning
At three we were in —
or were we out?
The chill was out the air was sweet
we must have been in
beneath the sheets the limbs the skin
the tender treats the honey
the lips the tongue, undone
The hours rocked us nearer sleep
but next to fleeting dreams
we touched and touched
until the day rose up
and we rose too
to coffee and tea and more love
in the garden
It might be with the paper goods
the bag of breads

the sweaters and vests that warmed
the guests as night rose up around us
It might be in the closet still
or in a drawer or in a tree
For all I know it might be here
beneath the cushion on my seat
The bra is gone but she is near
her breasts, exquisite nipples near
and free the sun or moonlight
near but it is gone
an absence quite indelible
as if its loss now threatens doom
appearing one dull afternoon
when meetings stir or neighbors pass
or those ex-lovers lounge on grass
It might rise up and scream, I'm here
I'm here, I've always been right here
beside you two in day in night
in love sweet love sweet acrobats
of on and off and in-between like shaking leaves
like wind like breeze like kisses breathing air
between two sets of lungs as summer breathed
It will appear, the question —when? and who
will fumble with those clasps
and will love last past light against
her neck her knees the moon the sun
my heart undone
and autumn in the garden.

AS IF HER BREATH

As if her breath
became air
the monarch
floating from lavender
to bee balm
my heart

KISS

Whether the mouth pressed to the wooden table
or sideways on a plate
might permeate more than a wicker stool's memory
of a pink geranium or the rosemary leaning into the glass
white light mid-afternoon and a green field
the snow tucked into the gray clouds the blue throat exposed
If the kiss held back for months sometimes asleep
sometimes dreaming might rise up to a treetop and wave
come home come back
even as the snow opens and the dogs hobbling on the road
recognize some signal a red flag or a patch of chokecherries
away from brick walls away from summer and waves knocking
my heart awake today
The kiss hangs from a high branch
a cloud behind a heart-shaped mouth
above the glass roof the green leaves the pink and yellow hibiscus buds
just about to open the orange lilies the delphinium
What if she stays there all winter watching the snow
build against the glass walls and the icicles hung from the corners
what if the green field never pulls her down or the sun tapping against
her hidden crease would I live from the wicker chair eyes fixed on the branch
my body red or green or yellow or cold awake or reason to sleep the light
just metaphor not nourishment or message as it slides over the birch
over the white pines and lands on the brown face that watches the sea.

WILL KILLED THE CAT

The cat woke up and
struck a deal
with death — her pulse
was worthless when
the sky was vexed
the day the night
held no respite
except for flight
when death was just a
hanging now — a longing
to set messes right
"I'll live if life is full"
she said "a conversation
touch, a way to love
and feel, to stretch —"
But death stood up
and shook her head
"Why should I help what I have fled
Here you invert the part that's mine
to live to learn or cut to bleed
not suffer as the suffering needs
the empty dish the sky-high bill
if you can't do it for yourself
try a handstand, try a trick
or try my style — the last sweet lick"
The cat looked out
and saw some sun
She stretched and said

"My life is done

my strength is gone

resilience shot

my love a fool, my angels not

and so if recompense or truce won't work with will

I will it not

there'll be another sometime soon —

a pattern etched from noon to noon"

Phrase complete she popped some pills

and swished the bourbon down her throat

her mind, a pitter patter maze

and then just daze that spread —

Her panic lost

her sorrow still

the willful blank

at willful cost

her life went stop

her death went start

and quiet too her tired heart.

ON THE SUBJECT OF SUICIDE

The apples and crabapples are in bloom today
the wood thrush sings
the cardinal sings
the woodpecker taps a code in the limb

Lilacs in bloom, furry leaves return
the dogs' full bark and hunt and hide
Helen of Troy, Helen of New Hyde Park
or was it Brooklyn, Queens —

Once my name was suicide
once my name was still alone
once my name was you and I
once my name was touch the tome

If she were with me a while
I'd think the days were yellow, bloom
but gone she is and ruined
through the long afternoon

Fuck she does with others, see!
holy am I, mama's turf!
see the way she plays with me
see the way she pouts and flirts

See the harmony with sleep
see she never counts me in

broken ladder, broken turf
halfway under, litany —

If I could speak out my full truth
mother speaks, she knows the ropes
pity, praise, admire me
under auntie's apple tree

Less than sparkle
more than fire
speak the truth
and called a liar —

Helen suffered tyranny
Helen wept and grass grew green
Job was she or wrath or blame
litany, a mother's shame

Once with grace she balanced true
impractical the steps she knew
when game is loss and loss is gain
crucify the slightest fame

Once when Helen watched the crew
speaking life and eating love
quietly she pushed to know
the secrets of those luxuries

Once was fire once was sand
once was seaside once was land

twice was silver thrice was gold
dancer lost and dancer sold

Here among the mendicants
birds will chirp and dogs will roll
peepers screech and old trees bow
all the wicked hands of blame

Helen was a dancer once
on streets she pointed practiced toes
on lawns she leapt and roses grew, peonies and daisies too
but mother silent never knew

Birds against the feeder rock
gurgle tenderness and gloom
holy holy holy rock
her soul along her silent doom

who lost the strength for mystery
and placed the bag over her head
then drugged
released her servitude

As silence sang near pitch and true
a tune she hummed when life was new
and no one else — not you not me —
knew Helen's saving melody.

CONTRA DANCE

I am a pariah
my lovers are liars
that's how we are wired
through lies and our scorn

I am a pariah
my voice is not tired
I shout and I shout
until others are blamed

Just call me pariah
I hate my entire
self as I hate
my entire name

My family twists away
friends twist with speed away
I am a liar and cruelty
my game

I am a pariah
I look quite retired
circles and circles
beneath each blue eye

as shadows or winter
fall like sharp splinters

and pin me to others
so docile this game

Now truth my reminder
though bitter the flavor
as arrows to quarrels
can't quiet this pain

And I am a player
I act like a player
I spin and I spin till
you call me insane

But first say pariah
when small smiles retire
and no trap can catch me
for what truth I am.

HER LONG SPINE

Once the sky was white, the narrow necks of the trees white too
leaves shook, silver and blue, summer was an old dream
only winter clasped love around the windows, tricking birds to angels
every hope for rescue stopped by the treetops
Smoke, just the dead girl
sitting straight at the gymnastic show
All the mothers with sprayed hair saw her long spine
but the tunic was perishable fabric
blue as an eye, blue as her face
Once the world savage and sweet whispered her name
whispered dead again, the flies dying too, winter
only the ladybugs survived and outside chickadees and jays, the proud pines
when the chair was green as a dollar and the Hawaiian skirt hung in the light
as if she might return as if trees were more than heat and decoration
I knew a woman — cruel and injured
she shot judgments from her mouth like pellets against the deer
I saw the injury, built a brown wooden room around her
filled it with light and pillows, colors and books
she lifted a pen and wrote a life or two, stretched and left the room
suspicious of happiness she lived as a cruel hand
Perhaps she knew the ugliness of touch as a child, perhaps not
something kept happiness away even with a pen in hand
though distracted by other mouths and eyes she wandered, set in her ways
I lived beside her for a while, took on the projects she began
hating the thought of abandoning even some thread —
perhaps the treetops understood more than the sky even though the sky
got the credit for the shifting color and breadth
I dug a deep hole on a warm November day

I threw the heads of dead sunflowers in

then wrapped myself in a down quilt

and climbed on top of the seeds

My cousin died with a bag over her head

She was fifty, ahead of me

I think the cruel sad woman loves sadness, spins it like a top

I love wood, cool warm on fire or high —

Just where the snow begins the tree ends

Just where the cruelty starts my sorrow lifts me up to the chimney

and lets me see the view: there are the dogs there is the white house

the two cows and the goats; there are the red squirrels in the leaves and the jays

there is the snow

Remember the brown hill, the ugly building, the telephone booth, the cafeteria

there are the dirty floors, the dirty bathrooms

I can lie in my comforter with a view from lower than the front door

see everyone pass by as if I'm dead — an entire life filled with strangers

Perhaps wood might save me if I had a box or if I had a branch to rest on

if I understood the finch and the chickadee and the crow and the entire view became what I loved

    and wished for

though the sight of a mouth, the memory of a scent

my friend or the dogs lying side by side at night —

Sometimes everything hates me — the geraniums

the bloody-mouthed hibiscus, the lamp, even my favorite pen

Sometimes it means dead to the world, leave the world be

you are dead dead dead sometimes that's who I am

Sometimes I watch from the chimney and count all the lives I knew

the houses I left, the books I loved and the children —

remember the friends down the hill when the body around the straight spine

was fat and afraid and the front door kept desires simple as magazine stories or novels

or a red flannel shirt soft as an extra skin but warmer, locked away

No one asked for anything except the two youngest children

with cards sewn in their pockets — but still that was fabric

not an evening melody or some pressure called greed

The house stood, made of tin, with a mother cut out of paper

and a father who chewed his dinner as if it were entirely different from the one

cooling on the kitchen table two hours earlier

Remember the richness of childhood

when the cut and scrape of the bark burned in a wonderful way —

to feel texture and heat even upside down, the branch and bark cutting

into the place behind the knees — and the tin house crooked

the sad faces smiling, the mica shining from the rocks

leading up to the front door in snow or feathers falling, always red

summer, when the leaves covered my eyes, leaves to hide behind and hold

That's when words fell against the birch trees and the pines

they promised steadfast love thicker than paper

each one pushed me through childhood up past the snow

Here I am on the chimney looking down again

there it is, a family, each face turned from the one beside it

here I am in the feathered quilt, I can see every foot that passes

the silver snow falls and turns to feathers

it covers up each print and the green grass

everywhere the snow falls, I measure the seeds beneath me

here where I am alive.

SECTION
TWO

COMFORT KILLED THE CAT

The cat woke up and shined her shoes
she brushed her hair
she blew her nose
she climbed a tree
and snatched a bird
and jumped back down
for her dessert
The cat with relish
drank some milk
she stretched
she yawned
then went berserk
The moral of this skinny tale:
if life's too cush it may get stale
and then all grace and ease may stop
the good before your time is up
From high upon her favorite pine
the cat jumped into branches fine
reflected in the pond below
then chug a lug a lug, she sang
and choo choo choo
it's time to go
So much for hair so much for shoes
so much for meals and her clean nose
when ease is all and all is it
comfort may invert and tip you
on your unsuspecting head
Then like the cat

who thought she saw
familiar branches under paws
the ripple of reality
will kiss you and then crack your knees
or offer you a dire disease
TB or AIDS or cancer, too
when comfort gets the best of you.

OCTOBER POEMS

ONE

A simple concrete room
then beyond the open lawn
far across the country where the whales sing
leaves tumble as if their scrape and drop might ward off footsteps
or the frames that carry danger
Through the glass ceiling of the conservatory at night
I see stars, I am protected by the glass walls and simply safe
the spirit touches my chin
so that I look up slowly to watch the universe —
During daylight the leaves spin and shake
their momentum frenetic as a heart
Sometimes I wonder where your gaze drops, after the pink caverns
after the supper among strangers, your current lover tossing quips
across the table — I am always in the boat dipping the oars
into the red water, tilting my head back to see the cedars and the pines upside down
the reflections loyal in the water, the weeds swaying
First the month of train crashes, then the month of window ledge, broken wall
broken hand, the light gleaming from your hand under the moon behind the sycamores in the park
I never understood my own capacity for damage until I knocked the door ajar
or was that the angel arriving with convection in her pocket?
Listen to the cadence of a broken pledge, once the orange chills to brown
as the snow locks us in —
There in October, the carpet's dismal gray, a texture I posted against my skin —
oil on my skin once your hands on my skin now branches firm as longing
as the fire burns less tenderness than duty, or the paper, kindling, logs so bright the stars
confused through the glass and the blue horse points out the window at the passing storm

a storm as temporal as flight, luminous, meager, nothing like the I am I am of the door
unlocked or the turtle slowly crossing the road to her nest knocked in by curious boys—
so much to do and who to put the finger on? The faucet's neck, just melancholy—
the fly, the constant motion, tilt or sway of trees without clouds to protect them or
parents guarding their feet—what about the warmer depressions where the bloom
continues, defying the season's instructions, like any ordinary child
What about the days when each current of air signaled loss or love, stilled the famous look
downward as the walk beside the leaping goats—the goats like a comedy act
and the tender faces of the cows, the farmers' daughter waiting for the school bus
as the light lifts up from the ground, her wave the only look of kindness, direct—
what about that insinuation or the dog's slight smile?
I remember a time when light was every sign of touch and touch a show of influence
a mark against confusion, a teacher or a mother, the lined skin beside the mouth an invitation
my lips my fingers every breeze, passion, standing on the stone wall facing west
the wooden shield where I looked at you through the camera lens and shot
the truest stillness from the room, the last touch of tenderness I saw in you
Now I think about your face against the carpet, a parking lot outside, the children
rushing to classes or suppers and your legs spread and my head resting there
taking in whatever salt and slick delirium my mouth briefly invented
there where the spiny pods covered the yard or the wooden palms of the dock
or the cool metal side of a rowboat, as the train rushed beneath that bridge signaling
gone gone and disobeying I moved toward and far away; now I am hidden beside
red branches and an early snow, stones stacked up against the goats and windows wide
wide facing west where we lived once, an open desperate clasp in a throat of drink
and food and fucks to set the walls on fire, which filled with hatred finally
though still your skin still your cunt your hands your face return to me
as another storm slowly drifts to the east and occasionally I see small
segments of sun before the owls begin and night breaks loose again.

TWO

After the wind pulled the leaves down, torrents of rain
against the tin roof then the pond amazingly clear
one frog on a stone the koi down beneath the leaves
the dogs digging up the brick patio after some sound or scent
roses falling apart glass holding light inside blue jars
the dragonfly balanced on the old root the snake skin wrapped from the root to the sage
Where did the glass floats travel? In what seas did they hold the nets up toward the sky?
Here the flat sky saying, winter, get your wool socks ready
get your sweaters out and the birches turned to skeletons
Once a finger against the neck or lips against the wrist now coffee and a car door
the exhaust following her up the road past the goats on their morning walk in the sun
past the three cows always leaving always doors and my chest hollowed out
always the most restless demanding out or there and away
briefly the body she said, how can you keep making love when it's only your mother
you're after — everything reduced to that
and the few stoic leaves still holding
next to the spiny stretching limbs.

Always the front door opening and closing the blue station wagon out the driveway
up the street and left at the park or down the road and left down the steep hill somewhere
out there a great flushing open world or a place beyond the dark trees and the pressure
of the water against the knees as the cars drove by a highway or another neighborhood
dangerous the entire world ominous and without protection
somewhere other parents holding the shoe box safely
but there the road off and the pressure too great to simply sit on the orange couch
and hope for nothing terminal though so many thought it was the perfect sitcom
a quiet open kitchen blue with cupboards and the maid's coconut candy wrapped to send

to her own little daughter far away she made her frilled dresses and missed her
had the photograph with her long dark legs and shiny shoes by her bed.

Would you say he's leaving now? would you say that a western state for a month means
that sort of change? or the hike through the Alps that kind of break as she went to China
was that the same abandon or simply looking for footprints to fit her shoes? Always that
silence or let me tell you about my day and she does by the end of the conversation exist
for herself as she wouldn't otherwise without you perhaps she disappears but you disappear
without her too — though your slot for detail is nothing next to hers but you're younger
and she earned the time all the hours of carpools a life of carpools and meals and the semblance
of order beyond the garden beyond the small brick path
Where did he want to be other than younger?
Really he might have chosen any other place a woman or a man but this is what he took
or asked for and here you are beside the mailbox waiting for the school bus a pine tree across
        the way
and the porch where the older boy keeps the cats he kills to dissect in his basement lab
you like his sister blonde and known to ring doorbells and run away
the girl born on the same special day as you, exactly your age give or take
a few hours, the girl your parents feel is unsuitable, unseemly, uncared for —
and you wonder thirty years later, did she have a mother?
knowing suddenly she did not — her father was a famous guitar player and the brother, perhaps
        a scientist —

There in your own backyard with the bronze boy on the dolphin, you call him your brother
his name, Timothy, you like to ride the dolphin with him and sometimes balance yourself
on his green head, a statue as permanent as whatever your young life has known
more so really than your mother's transparent skin, her hands barely made of flesh
so light they hardly exist unless they squeeze a reprimand or push into dough — off to
        the League
or a library trying to drive beyond yet her shell was so thin how could she ever step out of it

Today the birch leans toward the telephone wires and the pond miraculously clear after
the storm — you are drawn to the pile of stones by the garden's edge, where the fawn
got stuck last winter, where the goats occasionally cross over.

Wood to burn or rot, build homes or burn homes or a fire for warmth or the shelf
carved, the floorboards, carved, all the old names stacked never a permanency to keep
anyone always the sky between you and the others or a raging quiet
when the door shuts this time the last you say to yourself
tears pushing up behind your face always the end it feels so utterly unbearable
and everyone you've ever loved like this, prone to amnesia —
forgetting your name forgetting your quiet premonitions or your —
no first they put on the coat, barely out of bed and out they go for the run with
the ex-lover or the drive into a simpler place, and you wonder if you carry that
tinny noise with you even when it feels as though you don't speak perhaps you are still
making noise perhaps the tell-me-I-am-alive still runs out of your mouth like some slop you
    couldn't hold down
like some drool you can't reach to wipe off and you didn't even know it was there
Who knows you, really? the stack of therapists with their pads and little jottings do they
remember who you are? who knows you? that old scornful friend afraid of skin and drawn
to the church? the one who makes a living now through touch but never passion —
none of the lovers remember your shoe size they have their own lives —
yet you remember theirs — 7½, 8, 10 — and their favorite colors — what difference
does it make? the loneliness that pushes inside solitude
the heat beside the foot at night the edge of the pond colors from the wind appearing
like fish or spirits or Seurat come for a visit — or Monet — here you have your own
water lilies and Muriel sings the Water Lily Fire and the leaves rattle around.

It is October, your life is changing you feel it change each time you see yourself
in a window, another sleep or thinking about the girl raped at gun point
across from your old home, two miles from where you were raped all the knives

hanging from the pockets, but this time your mother believes it and she is afraid

you've already gone through twenty-six years of fear since that fall day, just about this time

of year in fact September, hating that new school and the born-again classmates —

wanting some edge as you hitchhiked home, a foolish day, truly loneliness and anger all

     over again

Alive you wanted to know if you were alive — well let's think about it in the back of a brown van

as the bikers swing their legs and tell their gang-bang stories — alive? you've wondered since

if there are ways to prove it or prove it to your father perhaps

because he still can't get over his brother's death — such a future and the unions, political

yet down he went into the dark scum of the Atlantic, fifty years ago on the cargo ship —

he died and you are named for him, wondering all your life if this flat air is why he enlisted

so much fear so much fear so little touch or kindness too dangerous.

Yes, love, keep it at bay if she moves closer she will leave you flatter than before this way if it's

only a ten-minute cup of coffee, the leather jacket on from the time she walks down

the stairs half asleep this way as the car starts up and the fumes lift around her in a dramatic

flare it's a small leaving, it's simply her way nothing personal in fact the sweeter it is the faster

she leaves in the morning — she says she can't help herself and each time your chest

hollows out and each time the dogs react less, but there you are

thinking of your mother and your father and that brick house

and every week it's more painful, not more ordinary as it might be for some

So you swear you'll move away from her more harshly than she moves away from you

you'll call the shots now you'll be too busy to get it fired up and then the wood will start

     to burn

this time perhaps you'll find comfort in a temporary house that already you've begun

to fall in love with — a temporary house and leaving, that will be another season

your heart buried beneath the garden somewhere and they can't leave you, the earth that is

or the walls as simply as waking up in the morning and lighting up the old routine —

simply focus on the birch trees and the lines running down its limbs and wonder

how that one line looks so much like a dragonfly and here you have one stunned dead

on your desk, enormous, and the lady at the orchard said transformation as you described them
landing on you all summer long—transformation on the wooden surface beside you
and there on the left limb of the birch tree like a branch as the sun goes falling falling
    and routine
bores you yet you long for the safety of walls and dependable seams
as each side loyally holds its neighbor up.

MISS MARY MACK MACK MACK, ANOTHER VERSION

Miss Mary Mack Mack Mack
all dressed in black black black
with silver buttons buttons buttons
all down her back back back
She asked her mother mother mother
for fifty cents cents cents
to see the elephants elephants elephants
jump over the fence fence fence
They jumped so high high high
they reached the sky sky sky
and didn't come back back back
till the fourth of July ly ly
this is a lie lie lie

Miss Mary Mack Mack Mack
all dressed in blue blue blue
jumped over a fence fence fence
to tell the truth truth truth
when she was up up up
she saw a bird bird bird
my feet it's true true true
are just absurd urd urd

When she dropped down down down
she hit the ground ground ground
and in one moment moment moment
was one small mound mound mound

A bit in shock shock shock
her mama screamed eamed eamed
If my young Mary ary ary
is gone I'll cream cream cream
that circus man man man
who caught her eye eye eye
and ruined my picnic icnic icnic
on the fourth of July ai ai

This is the truth truth truth
It is no spoof spoof spoof
Birds really lift lift lift
above the roof roof roof
but trusting girls girls girls
who don't accept ept ept
that they have feet feet feet
to stay erect erect erect
and try to fly fly fly
without their wings wings wings
will simply die die die
like stupid things ings ings

If girls accept ept ept
just what they are are are
and walk or jump jump jump
into a dump dump dump
they will survive ive ive
for a long time time time
as slugs or worms worms worms
unless they fly fly fly

which will belie lie lie
their bones and spine spine spine
though some have done done done
some tricks with gum gum gum

All mothers should ould ould
learn to use wood wood wood
in case their child ild ild
is swept with vile vile men
or runs away way way
and tries to stay a-way
instead of wash, cook, clean
and go to school ool ool
the wood will help elp elp
keep them in line line line
or catch the circus ircus ircus
man in time time time
to prove don't try try try
to tease or fly fly fly above
my girl girl girl
she is a pearl pearl pearl
and pearls are dear dear dear
and sometimes chip chip chip
when circus men men men
present false schticks schticks schticks

Miss Mary Mack Mack Mack
was put to rest rest rest
with all the rest rest rest
who tried to test test test

their natural ways ways ways
their ups and downs downs downs
their this is sky sky sky
and this is ground ground ground
she could not fly ai ai
she cannot walk walk walk
and now she's dead dead dead
she cannot talk talk talk

There is a moral moral moral
to this sad tale ale ale
don't be impressed essed essed
with fancy dress dress dress
or you may leave leave leave
your life behind hind hind
and live or die ai ai
like one lost ghost ost ost
it's true of many many many
don't make it most most most
be true to you you you
or you are through through through.

ARE YOU MY CAKE
TO EAT AND LOVE?

Are you my cake?
are you my cake?
I love your eyes
brown as the sea.
Are you my cake
to eat and love?
Your lips your lips
are food to me.
I want you, cake
and eat you up.
Your nose, a little buttercup.
Are you a cupcake
frosting sweet?
I do love cake.
I do love you.
Your brown eyes, meadow
green eyes, blue.
Your filament voice
your gurgle of rain.
Are you my love?
are you my cake?
Come here and let me
frost your face
as you frost mine
in winter, spring.
Oh my! your hum
is hardly sweet

your tone so rough.

No cake today.

You are so mean

words spin like fans.

I'll cut myself

if I stay near.

You may be sugar

but not here inside that boil

that bubbles up.

If you are cake

then eat you up.

I love your face

your red-shell ears

your snowy voice

and brown-sea eyes.

But when it comes to

sweets and love

you're more like steak

or black-bear stew

with chew and chew, less pillow

pouch, less curlicue.

You're tough, not cake

and I like cake

with frosting and a message, too

like, I Love You or

E Luvs J.

That effervescent milkiness

that sometimes pulls your bark

apart feels like chocolate

lemon cream or coconut

my cakey dreams!
Each layer stacked
each mouthful moist —
It's true I do prefer soft cake
my beefy pet, my moose, my glue.
How my jaw aches
from loving you.

CAT'S DREAM: PRAISE KILLED THE CAT

"If you're that hungry, I'm sure you'll die;
it's an accident that you're alive —"
said one big cat to another little cat
who sat on a tree with a tall tall hat
attached to her small furry head.

Once I was a little cat
and a big cat came and whistled out loud
"You're a brilliant cat you're a crackerjack cat"
and hollered till my heart felt proud
A brass band played and a float passed by with a papier-mâché bust ten times my size
Cymbals crashed and trumpets blared, children shouted and dogs chased tails
I nodded and I bowed with my tall tall hat tilting down in a regal display
"A genius folks, a spectacle!" said the big cat from her megaphone
and everyone on the curbside cheered
as I cocked my tall tall hat and said
"Bless you who loved me when I was a small cat
bless you bless you who loved me long ago
and curse the ones who loved too slow"
Filled with pride I swung and swayed and shook and stamped
with joy ablaze till lo and behold so clapped with praise and cherished
I collapsed, astray
Then nothing but the float and the streamers lay
my tall tall hat from a low branch waved
I was merely a mass of soft gray clay
shocked dead from the joy of one good day
praised dumb, I simply fell away.

THAT DAY

Every surface became part of the body:
the backs of chairs — breasts hips
lamps her open mouth
doors her tan back
vases the arches of her feet
leaves of the geranium
the glass bowl stones out the window
the open field the breeze rattling branches and leaves
surface of the walls
vines wrapped around the maple stump
On the lawn the heat
grass tickling my shoulders
sky wide as the space between us
connecting heat to her open mouth
her eyes shut
at night when air becomes
her hands my hands moving
over every surface of the house touching her
Once I found a mouth to kiss
kissed myself awake as I pulled
her down among the stones
beneath birch and pine
all greed or such hunger
No hand firm enough no tongue
wet enough to cover or fill each edge of space
the lines on her chin or the open eyes
or the silver ring covering her finger
Alive the throat wants more

fingers mouth her body against my cunt

her cunt against my arms neck breasts legs

full tenderness as if just the texture of skin

might relieve the heart on fire

Once the day opened its eyes

cast light and shadow over my feet

there she was sun

there she was the pear tree

there the peaches green hanging

from the tree there my belly

over the backs of her legs

Once the stars light and chance

once breeze calling love into every room

Once the links between each lover

fear rage suspension

then the morning held fog

soft as her breath

the suggestion of tongue the permanence

of loss etched into my shoulders

there she goes and the next

always the first

never just chance caused by longing

Every color some emblem of skin

some texture or radiant desire

Frozen the light stops

at the center of summer

the moon white in the blue sky

storm clouds pushing in from the west

As if heat from her legs covers the field

places its neck open to her mouth

or the lightest surface of her fingers
over the rim each turn
when the hummingbird circles the garden
nectar everywhere an echo of voice
sun over stones and there
where the sky leans against
her window some element of tenderness
cast like a shadow over her hand and we
move through the hours until night
and some reprieve when the wind pulls
lavender from the path and places it on
the windowsill her eyes shut
hours away and the moon above the rooftop
my hands as moonlight through her hair
lightly over her face
singing sleep and then desire or simply light
rising from the city streets as each morning
places our hands closer until she stands beneath
the door frame rain gliding along the glass
the bee balm steady as the wind shakes
Here the mountains lean our heads against
the surface of brush
every weather a vehicle for time her face
as I close my eyes her mouth as I
move through the day the trees
awake I am awake every surface some part of her body
she is everywhere.

A HORSE

Clip clop I hear a horse nearby
clip clop I feel my heart again
clip clop the sun breaks through the glass
clip clop let's have a little fun
not fierce not here too much
clip clop let's run hip hop
along the lawn
clip clop let's cut your hair my girl
clip clop against your neck the gum
is stuck a curve where sleep and mouth drops
wide clip clip let's cut it short

A whinny is that horsie, dear?
a whine a field a bale of hay
a whinny is that horsie or
your heart again at play?
I see the sky I see the trees
I see the goats beside the stones
the wires for the telephones between the trees —
Clip clip clop clop clip clop now dear
sit down now dear and stop your talk
just listen dear and listen well
now cross your legs and look at me
clip clip clip clop clip clop my love
and hear the tiger in my bones
my bones have always loved too much
roar roar my tiger sings
she sings as heat through glass

reminds me now of you

clip clip clop clip my love

Remember how the turnstiles stopped

when your hand passed into the room

clop clop oh horsie horsie stop and stay with me

clop clop I love your flanks

clop clop please cross your legs

your flanks clop clop I see

your head so smooth my

horsie legs smooth too let's

stop and stretch and rest a while

a lawn as green as your eyes dear

let's lie upon them touch and tear

let's tear a little too my

horsie dear — clip clop clip clop

come sit a while clop clop clop clop

come horsie low you know

you're safe inside my head

now rest as I unzip your flanks

my hands upon your hair

clop clop my horsie horsie dear

and touch your muzzle to my knee

clip clip I'll cut my hair short too

I want to be closer to you

clip clop clip clop my love

oh horsie rock back back then

forward dear clop clop my love

oh horsie dear oh horsie horsie

horsie clop clop clop

against the mountains or these roads

or woods or wood or will clip clop
or whinny clop or wind clip clip
my wind my horsie clop clop
sit and look at me clop clop
I think it's true
I'm sure it's true
I hear a horse nearby.

TIN

Some people know how to put themselves into a house

eyes set apart, nose steady, lips together, some silver snow inside the broken trees

Once a widow sat on a wood stove

cooked herself for supper then slept till morning —

wood, grass, something warm on the tin

all the woodpeckers lined up and hammering

The tin was simple as the snow and nearly the same color

and she never starved only a trace some piece of a breeze tucked beneath a flame

reminded her of other long necks and the fingertips she used

against those trees her skin was like that strips of birch

piled against the bricks everything drained of color

then the muted sorrow pink roses frozen brown

She ate when she was hungry and dreamed when she was not

tickled the belly of the long dog and wept when the kidneys failed

his long form pushed into an old freezer, still he waited for her still he's there in the basement

but she heats herself with scraps of hardwood, hopes the fire burns hot but slowly

even as the grass quiets the mess over the garden and comforting too the way that gravity

supplies the cover gravity and the red branches or the confusing reflections in the rippled

window glass gravity or a loss again still the fire sings to her and the hours

know her life is short and long the white line through the snow is a break in the clouds

not a future or a visit from an angel a still life or an apple or the circumference of snow

lifting above this crest where the goats hide even now when one fat piece of white light

cuts her head flat and her eyes appear thoughtful or in the midst of some reflection

Behind the wooden fence snow drifts down and the tin colored sky

with occasional breaks of light tumbles or passes over as everything

even the turkeys in the leaves, appears like mounds of refuse

breaks from the ground and waddles back toward an older home

still the morning glories cover some edge of memory the silver edge, temporal of course but pure inside and out though the stove ticks her face quiet from all the dim memories

Only the crackle of a ladybug landing on a wooden table reminds her of a true feeling

other than lift or sacrifice or rage something as real as tin so that this home might be real

and the chairs argue over comfort the sun will find her even when all the leaves have dropped

the orioles covering the tree on the crest of the hill will stay for her to memorize something new

something yellow though the color has loyally drained the color her health the future stretched

over the trees like v's of geese she has a few open months in a glass and wooden house

the cook-stove wood she'll feed herself, and sometimes branches like paintings

perfectly clear with a frame scattered for the birds, memory a chime cutting a melody

as snow blows over the field such a simple texture of hands in late autumn

patterns astonishing as tin, her throat filled with melody

those little tunes hummed in the daylight for her dead and dying friends.

STUPIDITY KILLED THE CAT

The cat rolled over and stretched in the sun
her paws two snatches of love undone
she pulled the light from the shadows in
then curled and mewed as the day wore thin
The day like others — a trained seal's song
yippee ya yippee yee, then gone
The cat liked patches of heat like fish
she yawned and she slept on her temporal rafts
and dreamed or dozed as if nothing would impose
wrath on the cat —
Violence, cruelty or death unknown
she prowled in the back of tacky bright homes
where sinister creatures roamed
"Ah peace," mewed the cat, "such peace — my own —"
Then out for a stroll for a snack and a chat with
a mouse or a chipmunk duller than a mat and flatter than a tack
tick smack slurp spat
As the cat prowled low a shadow swept by and covered the sun spots
like a simple black eye
then stomped the yellow from the lawns and the streets
and down one foot on the cat's fool beat
tick tock went her heart
then another stomp, stop
and the cat, so stupid
fright jostled her clock —
Out she ran toward a curve of heat
and into a heap on the ugly bright street
oh dumb dumb cat

so airy yet fleet — to never suspect catastrophe

as danger shimmied

and violence played with her obvious lack

of savvy tack and a tongue went slurp

and a throat went burp

and the cat was dead

without sun to stir her back again

to a drowsy sleep or her heart to beat

her pond-like chest

like the living rest

and peace was peace

though peace was least

in the shadow's crease

now that cat was done

stupid cat — naive.

A LIKELY STORY

Once I saw a monster in the water deep
She rose from the waves and called to me
Come here, little girl
come join me now
I'll love you to death
little girl, come out —
I looked to my left
I looked to my right
I called to my mama
with bumps of fright
but no one answered except
for the waves: splash splash
they sang, little girl behave —
So I knocked my shoes
from my little pale feet
and I stripped my clothes
to seal my fate
Come here, cried the monster
oh I love you truth
Come here, little girl, I'll comfort you —
Mama, once more I shouted aloud
and only an echo I heard resound
Kiss kiss, said the monster, kiss kiss
and hug; if you hold my toe I'll hold
your love, kiss kiss —
Into the water I swam, a child
the waves rocked over my head a while
and the monster waited from

her distant perch: chug a lug

chug a lug chug a lug—

The sky all blue and the trees

so black and the birds cried out

and the dragonflies slapped

their tails in the pond and the weeds

swept 'round and I swam and I swam

and I swam

The monster pushed her leg

in the air. If you'd like a good view

you can sit right there

she said as I treaded water, tired

I thought to myself, I'll soon expire

Then flap flap monster, she extended her paw

and afraid but exhausted I saw it was gnawed

Who bit you? I asked

A little girl last night

she said with a sparkle

and a giggle delighted to tell—

Oh my, said I, my heart my heart—

if I go with her pretty soon I'm not

if I stay where I am

I'll surely drown

I'm stuck and stupid and alone—

You're stuck, said the monster

you're stuck, little girl—if you

don't like me, swim back

to your family—

I'm all alone, I cried splish splash

my tears rolled down my little girl neck

splish splash splish splash

my mama's away

my family's left

The sun shone down, crickle crack crickle crack

the sun was yellow and the trees were black

the water was blue and the monster called

here, little girl, come to me —

Without much hope I climbed into her lap

flip flap went her flesh and the water went slap

flip flap she was wet and her skin all slip and she touched me

along my belly with the tip of her tongue

Tickle tickle, little girl, tickle tickle

I like you

thank you for joining me here, little girl

if you'd just lie back for a while

little girl I'll clean you off tickle tickle

then I'll feed you too —

Without much choice I stretched

my legs, I opened my arms

at my side, my head tilted back

in her lap, flip flap her flesh

and a little pool covered my back —

Don't be afraid, little girl, my dear

I'll clean you softly with my tongue

little dear, just close your eyes

and hum little dear and this bath

will be such fun tickle tickle little

girl, such fun —

I closed my eyes, I did what she said

I had no choice — it was this or death

so I started to hum as her pointy tongue
slid between my toes and over
my soles and up my little girl legs —
Tickle mama, little girl, what a hum
you are, I like that melody, fun you are
just continue until we are done
little girl; I'll clean you yes I will, little girl —
and pointy and soft went her tongue on my little girl legs
Behind my knees, she licked she did
then over my thighs in front, behind
then into my little girl shell she
cleaned and she cleaned and she cleaned
and she cleaned —
Then she turned me over with a
finger tip, she licked my bottom
flip flap all wet the pool was deeper
but the water was warm and it covered
me over like a slimy grass morn
or the cover that babies know when
they are born flip flap went her lap flip flap
She licked my left then she licked my right
mmmm mmmm, said the monster
you're such a delightful girl
little girl you're such a delightful girl —
She touched my back with her fingertip
up and down it traveled like a sponge all wet
it ran the curves of my spine and my sides
and over my neck then down again tip tip she cleaned
where she'd already been tip tip
tip tip went the monster — little girl

you're awfully clean—
Then over she rolled me one more time
and now I was coated with the monster's
slime so she started again between
my toes lick lick went the monster
lick lick—this time she traveled to my
little girl waist, she licked my navel
and my belly, she said
little girl you taste like the pond lick lick
and her tongue went up to my
little girl ribs lick lick she
covered each one little rib
and the tiny nipples on my little girl chest
just hum, said the monster I'm almost done, just hum—
Along my neck with her fingertip
she touched my throat, she touched
my chin, she touched my
nose, my eyelids—hum little
girl, don't be shy, just hum
hum into my ears, one by one—
Then down my arms she cleaned
and scrubbed with her fingertip and my
hands each finger then with her tongue
flip flap she sucked and my eyes
were closed in her lap flip flap
flip flap—
By the time I was washed
I was dirty again—from her lap
came a stream a smooth ooze it seemed
that covered me when she cleaned—

All ready all set all done, I said
monster I'm turning red, I said
now feed me, you told me
you would, I said, then she turned me over
of course, little girl — first course:
just suck this piece of me, little girl
it's in my lap, just me
little girl — it's very tasty and free
little girl, first course —
So I sucked and I sucked from
the monster's lap, face down
I sucked her soup like a bat
like a little girl bat
It's good, I said
Keep it up, said the monster
all day, she said, second course comes
when the first is through; I'm sure there's
some soup left in you — when
you're done I'll have yours then
we'll start with two — suck suck —
I sucked till my mouth and my tongue were tired
and my belly was full of soup
it's true, then the monster
lifted me up and sucked some soup
straight from my little girl cup —
Such broth, said the monster
such broth in you — you're
a meal you're a feast
you're a little girl stew —
Then I pushed her away

If I'm stew I'm through —
Wait little girl, I want more of you
No no that's it, I must go home
and I jumped in the pond
splish splash, my home my home —
Once I returned to the shore I knew
when hunger stirred I'd want more soup
and my life took a turn then
my toes all clean
and I knew in my heart I'd have monster dreams:
flip flap went her tips and her tongue went dream
flip flap
I lived my life with a jar of brine
to remind me of the monster's pond
and I learned to whistle the cleaning song —
I met soupy ladies
and showed them brine splish splash
I hummed when I dared and I hummed when I could
when taste was touch and touch was food
and the monster lived in my
heart crickle crack like the sun
when I needed to hum splish splash
Come home come clean come visit me
she sings from within and I try to be
good flip flap when my conscience allows me
to be splish splash — and the soupy ladies are free —
flip flap
monsters fierce are we splish splash
in our briny ponds are we splish splash

and our tongues our tips are deft
flip flap — come in for a midnight swim
splish splash the water's warm as can be
splish splash and monsters all are we
and monsters all are wee.

MORNING MANTRA

Fear of pickles
fear of beets
fear of kiwis
fear of leeks
fear of cabbage
fear of farts
fear of fascists
fear of hearts
fear of babies
fear of cats
fear of bridges
fear of bats
fear of wrinkles
fear of pudge
fear of ice cream
fear of fudge
fear of forests
fear of lakes
fear of cancer
fear of steaks
fear of slugs
fear of fish
fear of rapists
fear of ticks
fear of quiet
fear of noise
fear of yeast flakes
fear of joy

fear of nighttime

fear of ice

fear of sadness

fear of lice

fear of failure

fear of fame

fear of fat

fear of planes

fear of cornbread

fear of beans

fear of tofu

fear of dreams

fear of living

fear of death

fear of wheezing

fear of breath

fear of money

fear of none

fear of rodents

all fears done.

SOME THINGS CONTINUE WHEN YOU'RE DEAD

Some things continue when you're dead
Your bed, the ficus tree
the paneling on the wall
the pond outside the window
and the lamps beside the door
Even the dogs, your sisters, brother
who might mourn for a while
turn to look for you
returning home, then return
to their own lives:
the baby's curling fingers, the cafes
the books, the friends, the sky, the ground
Your couches, pale pink dishes, poems
blue bicycle, blue snowshoes
would find other homes
The papier-mâché turtle and the yellow bowl
all the details that once made the threads of you
You — would become the details of some other life
A haze might hold, held through the memories
the critical barbs, the indignation and the laughter
the evenings with the angels and the walks
along the hilltop by the goat farm
Perhaps life is just as tenuous as you dreamed
even with the extras like snow piled to the windowsills
fires burned to coals
the simple acts that kiss and sleep from one day to the next
the view of that gathering
paper clips, pens, a few notes and letters thrown against

the window tilted to the ground
the last view when the car turned upside down
on the road with hidden ice
Some things continue when you're dead
Even the car, that last embrace
the radio, tv, the tv shows
So when it's time to go or gone to come right back
keep it in mind, the threads, the rope
the boat and thank the ones that
offered added scope, some special language or a look
the fawn colored sky, the eggshell sunset
light that touched you differently
They will continue when you're not
so fill each up
the days are quite miraculous
when pulled away
and each dear face that looked but didn't look
until your ordinary life fell away.

SECTION
THREE

GREED KILLED THE CAT

The cat woke up and screeched
"I'm starved"
She grabbed a chicken from the yard
"I'll eat you all
feathers and lard," she hissed
" 'cause your time is up"
"I'm just myself"
cried chicken, fear
against her throat, cat's teeth so near
"I make fine eggs and chicks galore
My clucks are music
feathers pure and clean
a poet's dream machine
is what I mean
clu clu clu cluck"
"Who cares a hoot"
said cat, "not me —
I'd rather judge your symmetry
inside my mouth — you're food to me
publicity for ruthlessness!
my chicken oh my pudge"
Then Bark the dog leapt in the yard
"I'll let you go
with eggs, that's it —
this comes to plain respect
or death for you, sweet cat
sweet cat, think quick —
Fine chicken is a poet's dream

She makes those lyric cakes and creams
Devotion she is through and through
Now take some eggs and out with you!"
"An egg is not enough, dear dog
You know my appetite is large
no yolks or whites will fill me up
I need her flesh, the crack-oo-ling
that tickles my digestive dreams
Why give two hoots for longitude?
when chicken can increase my girth
and mirth — a simultaneous treat!
And don't forget my rep, dear dog
impeccable is what I mean —"
So cat took off with chicken's squawks
She jumped the fence and dined at once
Then Bark the dog let loose a growl
and pulled cat by her tail so foul
"My history is all I've got
I'm delicate, my lives too short
and you so harsh
permit me what I want"
said cat, "cease now, dog
offer your respect —
or you'll regret your insolence
and meddling
you canine ignora*mous* sap"
"I think not, cat," said Bark the dog
and snapped cat's neck
and spine against a pine
"A quiche might have permitted friends

but greed is greed and spells the end
for you who knew no compromise"
said Bark the dog, tears in her eyes
The foolish cat was dead again
and chicken who had lived to give
went down with greed — a penalty for poetry
the victim now and featherless —
cluck cluck alas lost innocence
While cat with feathers in her gut
was punished for her now last sup
bad bad bad cat bad greedy cat
and how the chicks wept through the night
An operatic hush upon the yard
was all that welcomed sunrise the next day
and Bark the dog paid her respects
beside a flock that pecked dear chicken's grave
then gravely pecked cat's sour remains —
Such penalty for greed left stains upon
those worn and somber lives
And still greed thrives —

RAIN

For Helen Weiser, 1944–1994

If the braids unfolded like a tree unfolding
leaves on the ground behind just blue
one split in the shelf but the rain has begun again
faster than a heart race keys of the typewriter
leaves in their falling dance turning color see the tears
who could tell the difference between tree and solemn face
waiting then shedding as the pines such arrogance
simple in their innocence broke and broke
the maples' spirit — selecting the crossed heels
hoping to avoid that hanging girl
flat black dancing shoes corner and the dust
the curtains transparent
the grass outside now covered in sun
while the burned house rebuilds itself
saws quiet on a Sunday
mountains blue, the imaginary sea
almost the same as the sky her head tilting
the mouth just opening
aimed at the ones who left her like this
see she is molded once spent a life trying toward acceptance
now that pride called failure

I saw a fence, the paint scraped off, I saw the apple trees
fruit dropped down, I saw a sky and the same
hilly ground — brown bottle sage from the mesa
sycamore of childhood, raspberries the lonely sun softening
as summer slips — see how her face stays

see how her eyes close with sorrow, the mouth
wise words hidden feels the shadow and the globe of her future
split across the center balances the shelf—
tears or water from that blue sea
mottles the plaster as she waits and nothing as the years change
or pines watch, cedar berries gathering along the trunk
trains, cars, planes, phones even the soles of her feet down on the floor
the fence broken but fresh white paint trying to hide the missing teeth
the rain falling and falling still softly
voices in the kitchen clatter hands when she was still daughter with a brother
touches and leaves and weather spiraling away roads and air, the lines dreaming
though the months invert and her mother will not speak her name

Broken daughter or record or doll
dancers stretching as the rain falls down
ring a rosy see the mother's seal
name forgotten or left behind
as the doctors and lawyers the teachers sit
for weeks they remember quirks such shame
a dirty woman such tangled hair
though never quietly holding their blame
and see she is waiting see still she waits
as one year passes and her feet are ruined
her mother covered as the rain falls down
leaves all golden or red or brown
the fence now painted and the pines still cruel
overlooking such stretch as taller they grow
now maples weeping their leaves fall down
and the burning house one light lit blue
now the fire quiet and the window glass new

the chestnut stump see the weeping leaves
here a daughter fixes her mother's food
see she bends still dancer though
her feet are gone her brother dreaming
sometimes shouts her name
so that moonlight sinking she remembers that home
now she rises as the moon when the stars drop tears
and they call her name as she tilts her head
as the window dares and her birthday nears
though her feet can't bend as her back can't bend and her hands
too red and her hair too tangled
for a proper lunch as she knows a mother
has a home and cousins as she quietly looks
but the talk just runs and the rain won't stop
yet they will not speak and she cannot see that they will
not come and her mother too as the red leaves fall
see the green to yellow see the yellow to red
see the red to frost as all silence sings
hear the silence sing hear the chords it calls
hear the mother's silence as the name just gone
claiming none no daughter no daughter no name
as she breathed and slept with skin to touch
and red hands warm when the voices came
hear the voices' silence hear the way the rain
against leaves and the leaves against the air return
hear the cars go by hear the telephone ring
hear the night drop down as the season changed
such love such love when she slept again
the house rebuilt the white paint dry
who loved and when

and they would not speak
who did she love?
and they would not speak
who sternly cast such judgment down
standing on the dirt or the mud or stone
as the leaves fell weeping
but it all may stop
now that silence reigns
and name or not she won't come back —
crystal or photograph, locket or chord
or a lock of yellow hair when she first fell down.

MONEY

Money was her father
and she kept it in her pocket
and she spent it when she raged
and she spent it when she roared

Money was her mother
and she kept the bills folded
in bundles in her pocket
the texture she adored

Money was a lesson
and she studied it with pleasure
she kept it as a treasure
she cherished it with love

Money was her monster
she showed it when she wanted
some protection from the world
like a bubble or a glove

Money held her interest
when with people interest faded
after fearing them or saving
her money was so dear

Money like a father
money like a mother
and money like a teacher
in a life quite queer.

LEAVES

After Robert Desnos

The handful of leaves thrown into the pond
simple as the sky in the pond
or the catbird perched on the white chair
Leftover rain shaking down then the leaves gathered
into a small pile and thrown in the water as a message
Perhaps she lives on the other side
perhaps the scrub pine and the rim along the pond's edge
are emblems of plenitude
perhaps the open palm the dull memory of limbs alive
pulled by the slightest suggestion of her scent
as she swims from one side to the other or out to the middle
Once when the leaves floated in a patch and the wind
knocked the rain from the branches, once, well
the sky took some up again
and eyes always assuming that the sky fell into the pond
saw it lifted up and the sky opened its mouth
and the leaves hung to the sky's tongue
On most mornings it's just leftover rain or heavy dew
the fridge hums and the clock moves round and round
The leaves meant I love her
the mark on her face like rain her voice the most
ordinary words covered my throat
Better to take the leaves off the trees or the car or the sandy
red ground feel the slip the veins and edges
place them in a stack, compressed and then release them
on the pond so that she might find them, they might
surround her in the water or miles away she might

in the midst of a telephone call or some language on a screen

or strangely in the middle of a dream at night

suddenly see leaves floating over the surface of the sky

Better than speech

Still morning, small waves unraveling and then rain

evaporating into air the last drops sliding down the windows

as if the palms covered were always open always emblems

Water or the surface of a wrist or a hip against my neck

speaking and there is the boat blue as the sky

the last veins of the leaf before it drops from the tree or the pond

against the leaf's surface or the rain as it circled the roof last night

the oaks shielding sleep from the storm and there is the dog's blue water bowl

reflecting mid-afternoon sun warming the water throwing diamonds into the water

around one leaf green perhaps my message returned

Her head lifting out a breath she pushes the water behind her

swims the wide circumference all the leaves dropped to the sandy bottom of the pond

or pushed along the edge of the rim

that I think of as I think of water or the surface of a leaf against a palm a foot

an arm extended pulling the body to the farthest side

Once when the wind placed the leaves on the surface of the sky

the sky filled the pond and she floated in the sky's wide mouth beside the trees

the leaves fell beneath the length of her body

her head tilted for air the pond a balance of blue and black

the motion of limbs and then release the clouds filled with leaves

everything upside down twice alive always changing

then clear as the kingfisher flew over the water holding a fish

she floated in the eddies beneath the shadows

and the leaves spun up and then rested brown green red against her arms.

GRANDIOSITY KILLED THE CAT

The cat woke up
she cracked her neck
then looked for a delightful snack
She headed for the kitchen door
and snatched a mouse from off the floor
Then taste buds sharp
she wanted more—
Cat liked mice pies
she loved mice stew
she cherished pickles
and puddings, too
"I think I'll eat until I drop"
she gurgled and then scooped one up
—a mouse that as she watched
grew large
with ears like kites and eyes less flight
than bite—
The cat amazed thought big is best
and bit this mouse like all the rest
"Oh mouse, you're huge
you're quite a bloke!
Where are your like-sized furry folk?"
"Just wait," the mouse said
quietly, "pull out your teeth
and follow me"
So cat with drool dripping in threads
followed big mouse with cheer
not dread

and mouse, pure calm and peace and joy
led cat into a Jon Swift ploy
where gathered 'round a tabletop —
ten mice the size of elephants!
"Oh dear dear mouse you're good to me"
said cat with glee
And just as cat pushed forth her claws
a mouse's tail knocked flat cat's jaw
then wrapped around her thick striped neck
and cracked cat on the tabletop
Then chomp chomp chew
and slurp dee do
"We like you, too," said one huge mouse
and cooked a pot of striped cat stew —
Oh cat, whose greed meant need and unfulfilled
was killed —
less brains than fat
less love than fat
though more than need
was cat's soft mew
before they chewed her up
and threw her bones onto a crop
of catnip topped
with cat's bad luck
Poor cat who in the face of feast
forgot the basic laws of beasts.

MY COUNTRY 'TIS OF THEE

All the linen on the tables, white dishes with roses.
Eyes closed: there is the copper beech
eyes closed: there, the Japanese maple
behind the stone house, at the edge of the upper field.
Once her hands were so light I wondered, paper? or leaves?
Yes — leaves — to leave, her eyes
closed; to leave, fear covering her teeth; to leave
they sold her or they watched her or they touched her or
she disappeared inside the steam of their breath.
My country 'tis of thee.
Of course medication to calm down or perk up
take the edge off
perhaps any feeling too much to bear; she believed or he believed
any failure worse than death.
On the corner my sister began screaming
crazy crazy you are crazy
in a Spanish town, my brother's wedding day
no one said: quiet
they said, stop bothering your sister; control yourself; you are selfish
you are crazy; sit down and shut up.
To thee I sing.
And she agreed: the air, foam, tangible
the simple request for a coffee in a cafe without them.
Love as a work of art: a sculpture, a mud pie, a bread
love as feathers or the buds beginning on the pear tree
or the caged finch trying to make a nest from
the ribbon hanging between the bars.
A blue morning glory, red geranium, white amaryllis

the lavender veronica, the oregano and sage hanging from the hook, a yellow kitchen
the tin buckets catching sap from the maples and the birch
smoke above the sugar shacks, the koi beneath the surface again
the orange bodies in the brown-green water.
How quiet on a Tuesday morning
wind and breath and the occasional hello from the caged bird.
My country 'tis of thee
sweet land of liberty
on a day like this — the dream of dying: the family
gathered; the black fabric, the weeping friends; the weeping husband
standing apart from the weeping daughters; the weeping son
standing by the door — to thee I sing —
lilac, magnolia, the bombastic entrance of spring.
A rainbow of sorrow painted across the chest:
save me save me live —
what do you need to breathe, mother; what do you need
to weave the future into the day?
A blue canoe? a yellow bicycle? a plate of matjes herring
and a loaf of black bread, sour cream, a bowl of soup
a chocolate covered graham cracker, a hand, open, motioning here —
stay — see the field see yourself beside the robins in the field
then a milkshake or then a bucket of fried clams or then
a temptation of laughter suggested by the blackbirds — all the buds
red green brown — yellow grass, the ice still holding to the wooden
board, the swan guarding his stones; the crows along the branches —
my country — here on the hill
ladybugs along the window panes, flies waking, covering all the edges
blue blue blue eyes; blue sky; blue morning glories, blue jays, blue birds —
If there were a magic potion what would it instill?
curiosity? the redwings' trill?

There—the crocuses, the daffodils begin, you see in death's warm mouth
it still continues—there beside the sea, homes on fire, lives on fire
children decapitated before their mothers; mothers raped before their children
—those people who want to live; today people beg for their lives.
And here, a flat condolence, such wishing on the part of the children and the husband
and her own wishing—let me die and be free.

The child sat on a brick path
wondering if her mother
was really gone or really there, still, in the kitchen—
nothing honorable about living; nothing spiritual about dying
sweet land of liberty.
The angels hold leaves: on the leaves, eyes; on the leaves, breasts
they look down from their pockets of suspension, beautiful heads with wings.
That lawn, the woods, the barn, the sky between the trees, windows
where sky—let me out let me out; is death a suggestion of love?
My country 'tis of thee
a dirty arm, a list of words
the desk covered with papers, the telephone on its side—
If there is a potion, swallow it:
a great compilation of desires, or a replay of childhood
sternly stand and move the wooden spoon in the pot: bones, beans, beans, bones.
Stir it, stir it, make the day light.
The mother sleeps, and this is a day of sun, the season changes—to thee
to thee to thee I sing.
She sleeps and wakens and her sentences are crooked
the words are inside out; the television shows an Italian movie
the radio sings Maria Callas; she sleeps again and the father lies beside her
watching the movie, listening to the opera, the air rage the air get it over with
the air control yourself, the air sleep, and the shaking body

sweet land of liberty, here on the hill, there is the meadow

hands covered in ink, speak, choose — to thee I sing —

breath, future, snow, purple buds, corn stubble up to our knees

leaves fallen beneath the sycamores —

my country 'tis of thee

sweet land of liberty.

Once there was a mother

she was very very tired

from the striped pink morning to the night sprayed with stars

she wanted to die.

All the children cried out, here we are here we are

the husband shouted, see them over there

and the mother shook; she wept

she put days into the car, days into the sink; days into the garden

days onto the desk.

Daylight opened the moon

the moon opened the sun

the world screamed kiss; the world screamed

love hate hate love failure failure stupid fool; she was so tired

the hummingbirds returned and whispered, sleep

they are grown or waken they are grown.

Sweet land of liberty —

choose us said the children

choose us said the redwings

choose me said sleep.

To end the poem, to let her speak

to let her leave

spring, bird song, willows, birch, sycamore, pansies, crème brûlée, strawberries

I cannot help myself

redwings, butterflies, hummingbirds, daisies, tulips
peonies, blackberries, night swims, milkshakes, chocolate
fried clams, potato soup, bicycle, blue canoe, I love you
to thee I sing.

WHEN FEAR WAS SMALL

I opened the door and saw through the screen
a band playing trumpets drums and dancers
colorful legs kicking into air sun on the steps and shade beside the trees
I stepped outside walked down the wooden stairs
followed the path to the center of town looked at the band more closely
felt the color and the rhythm snap my spine
till stars hummed among the marchers
Once when fear was small I covered myself: hat cape scarf gloves
and I watched the blown cheeks of trumpeters
the fast hands of drummers the fast high legs of dancers
as they marched through the streets of town
I stood behind trees
No one could see me the sound was marvelous the light
but I loved my dark home all the chairs I'd grown
and the tables and the scratches on the walls
I was small and fear was in and out and
I learned new names my language changed
until fear was large and shielded every view
even you were out of sight and silence clipped my tongue
she kept my fingers still sky was only blue music loud or soft
dancers fast or slow
and the sound in trees muffled my necessary heart
till I turned away and faced a wall
and once again my fear was small.

DOE SEE DOE! *(To be sung aloud)*

Spin your partner: doe see doe
Spin your partner: doe see doe
Round the dance floor you must go!
Spin your partner doe see doe!

Hearts to the rafters: doe see doe
Hearts to the rafters: doe see doe
Round and round and round you go
Hearts to the rafters: there they go!

Round and back and sideways go
In or out or the barnyard go
Steal a kiss or touch a toe
What a dance floor dancers ho!

Swap a right foot for a left breast
Use your mouth, you know the rest!
Up above the treetops go
Toward the moon: sigh and swoon

Practice stepping to and fro
Only that way can you go
Toward another without show
Round the dance floor go girls go

Check your heart: it's in the middle
Check your spleen: it's just below
No one sees the light that passes
Between leaps that spark these lasses!

When you swing your partner silly
Check the lady on your left
She's as tough as tender willing
Nothing less than one soft filling

Catch her eye; she's eyeing you
Catch her hand and kiss a few
Fingers thick or fingers slender
Think of how they'll spark your blender!

Round the dance floor: doe see doe
Do you know her? Does it matter?
If you kiss and buildings clatter
Grab some soap and start a lather!

Up to the rooftop: see lights flicker
That's because you failed to lick her
Drop to the dance floor with discretion
Steer away from lapsed regression—

If she has eyes like your mother
Or a mouth like one great-aunt
Or wide hips like those past lovers—
Switch with haste, don't start to smother!

See past partners in the corners
As they fondle their new lovers
Let your heart rise up not splatter
These are normal dance floor matters

As the music rises, falls
And you see another taller
And you shapely feel much smaller
Don't begin to scream and holler

If this big one blows your heart
And her fingers grind your blender
Twist your head and let her lead
Pass the reins to your new steed!

Live with care but not much thought
To the swiftest lust surrender
Round the dance floor: doe see doe
Switch your partner: there you go!

Switch again! Here comes a real one
Filled with heartbreak filled with weeping!
See the cheeks, now see the chin
Feel the way your blush begins —

As you swing your newest partner
Into hands of that lost lover!
Nothing slows when dancing flatters
Hearts can't quiet lust's bold laughter!

Try the dance step faster! faster!
Maybe that way you can catch her
Doe see doe, then bow to your partner
Not too low or hands may falter!

Bow to the left then the right then the middle
Clasp your hands to the shapely fiddle
Look! the dancers in an uproar
Someone's screaming on the dance floor!

Use discretion, ladies please!
All improper gestures ruin
Fun for partners past and present
Out the barn door bad girls go

Take new partners for the moment
As the music quickens, slows
Catch your breath and drop your shoulders
Feel the music as it flows

Now don't forget your origins
Be polite to those old partners
Bow to the left to the right to the middle
Doe see doe to the newest fiddle!

Gosh! some sneaked back to past partners!
Under floorboards — hear the sighing
Could it be that I am lying?
Could it be that tongues are thriving?

Hearts on the ceiling sighs below
Then sighs on the ceiling and lone hearts go
Bigger than a bread box smaller than a shoe
Swing your partner: round you go!

Look! here comes the sun: arising
Listen! hear the roosters crow
Swap your house keys, now your car keys
This is how all dances go —

Kiss the hand of your old partner
Tongue a new one soft to splendor
Study neckline, adjust bias
Till the next dance love her whole!

Swing your partner: morning's here now
See you next month for our barn dance!
Let your dance steps and your heart strings
Loosen as the shadows show

One last time around the dance floor
Then a bow to the music low
And out the door into the new light
Love your new life! Joy girls show!

(hum the melody)

Round the dance floor, up to the rafters
Under the floorboard passions scatter

Never question what's the matter
Let those passions pitter patter!

(hum the melody)

Round the dance floor: doe sees doe
Round and round and round she goes
Never wondering never wiser
Round and round and round girls go!

ALCHEMY

The trees shake and the pond, flat as the deck, is nearly still. The chill in the air suggests that perhaps the new woman loves you. Or perhaps your sorrow is too enormous. A bouquet of sorrow still hidden for her to find, for her to love or leave. Body of sorrow hands of sorrow breasts of grief. When you make love some transformation lifts you into a neck of peace. To maim, that longing to slice your arms, your face or neck, just an extension of the time you need to write to feel alive on paper, to accept the ugly landscape that you are.

The treetops stay along the pond. You light fire after fire but can't get warm. The deck is cold again. The sun is gone and there is that road from the dream years ago after winding over the New York border, driving toward the house along the sharp dropping rock, along the mountain edge. You want her soft eyes. You want her hands. All the tears resting in your chest. Let them go let them go, open your eyes, mouth open, let the tears out.

In the moment of waking, the dog, guardian of heart, is dying. You do not look at her slowly disappearing face. The one who cared for you, who traveled by your side from state to state, home to home, lover to lover, is about to leave. You cannot say this silently or bellowed into the speechless walls. Fear gathers like thorns against your tongue. In the early dying you cannot speak to her. You will not see her leaving. You believe that she found this new love to take her place. Desperate for continuity, for immortality, you believe that it is her kindness in the form of a woman, her love in the shape of a new mouth.

Silly that you cannot quietly fold yourself around the one you love, the one who, years in pain to stay beside you, begins to die. That soft body, those eyes, the lopsided hips and red collar. You have tried to turn her into a woman and the trick will not untie itself for years. Such determination to make the crooked even, to be safe. But the living cannot assume the soul of the living. It will be someone else, something else, and only when you place sorrow's noose around your neck and hang and hang for the breeze to bring you into the quietest hole of memory, nothing more than memory and ashes and desire for texture as weather or wool or fur or skin.

Your memories and ink on paper are your only home. So yes she dies and the next year her sister dies too, as again you look elsewhere, still afraid of releasing even those ridiculous illusions that you created, those strategies to get you through hours or weeks. As you begin to let yourself feel slowly, as you let the ink move on the page, she is there and not there. They both are. And the woman who holds the great weight of immortality, she is fallible and mortal and she could never be what you hoped. It was impossible from the start, a woman with the soul of a dog. Bathed in death's kisses, she is a woman with a pinecone in her mouth, herself.

The white sky falls into the pond like ice and another day drops through the trees. The air is cold and your hands are stiff. The new love drives toward you and all you care about is the heat between her legs folding over yours and the heat of her back and the sweat against her chest and her mouth, the tongue moving slightly in and out. The phone dead for the second time in three days, and the hours settle against the leafy edges of the pond, fall returned.

The basement open, closed, in dreams or memory or here beside the pond. Leaves hold onto bayberry, the oak, as if summer might still keep them safe. The entire world leaving and you love her and you try to pull that love apart because something in it seems, for extended moments, to make you whole. It's not that the poetry is gone and your life has disappeared in two months, it returns and her kindness fills you with salt, and now you must let the tears go, and you are afraid, here in September in the cold dream.

The chickadees eat their sunflower seeds and they calm you. The new puppy sits in the car chewing a bone. The blue jays peck at the wooden benches, and snow gathers above the trees. There is no easy way out and no easy way in. There is the pond. There is the ocean. There are the scrub oaks and the bayberry. There is the memory of the walk on the beach, collecting shells and the shark's head. Death followed you home and the dog died in a night of convulsions. Her shaking body, perhaps wanting to stay, perhaps wanting to leave. And desire, an alchemical attempt to try to turn through touch and sight and smell the dying into the living, the dead into the living, the living into the dead.

The flying squirrel is scattered on the snow, pieces of fur. Her body now part of the fox. Snow falls and covers the tracks, covers the kill. But memory and dream are holding proof; scent, a true print of fact. The scent of basement, the scent of girl, the scent of the face in the window, the scent of fall tumbling from the sky into the pond, the scent of the lover stepping toward the door at dusk, stepping on the pine needles, the fallen leaves of the oak, and the scent of the dog, as you held her shaking body through the last night and cut a handful of her fur to keep in your pocket, more like a pellet now from your constant touch, proof that one being saw the ugliness in the landscape and still loved you.

THE CAT ALIVE

The cat with pomp
licked clean her hair
she watched the light
upon the stair
descend as if some force
were there —
dead foes dead friends past lives
She saw an apparition then
it motioned to the ceiling once
it blew a sea breeze by her head
"I loved you once
now I am dead," she said
"I know so few," cat purred aloud
"my life one track of do it all
the chase the kill the meals the sleep
and then my vices, comforts, too
but rarely love; now who are you?"
The apparition swept a tail
along the crests of light that fell
then curled around the puzzled cat
a blanket or a shadow there
"Remember years ago," it said, "the way
the moon would speak to you
would touch your whiskers
touch your toes
remember how your heart would
grow when night would sweep you in its cup
and tumble you through joy a while —

Your fur so bright in that moonlight —
What was it that inspired you?"
The cat sat up and stared with dread
"I've no more lives," she said with dread
"you're just a trick," she said with dread
"you want to stomp me dead," she said
"No no," the apparition cried
"don't let your fear propel such lies!
Think carefully to find the key
to life to peace, mortality —"
"I touched a flower once
and it touched back," replied the cat
"I saw some birds fly from a tree
and I climbed onto branches fine
to find their nest
like all the rest it made me wonder
loyalty? or flattened possibility?
I always hoped to fly
so rather than consume the family upon return
I asked them for some flight advice
and generous they offered me
some feathers and some tar
then showed me how to fly
not far then how to land with grace
Those birds were kind —
I met a thoughtful thinker once
she sat in sun and tried to elevate
my instincts to a cloud, but I fell down
Happiness would come to me
and levity held me then

and comfort got the best of me
like bars that hold the sweetest zoo intact
I've witnessed love, the lift and swing
the heat that emanates from two who waddle
wade or leap inside a mirth that from this skin
seems weak—"
The apparition stretched and said
"Your loyalty your life, not much—
where is the passion pulled from some
undone or when the rise and float began
some source some word some touch some clue
where is the confidence that buoys
integrity the truth where is the best of you?"
The cat with anger backed away
and started toward the door
"To see you here
means life no more again
please go away I want to stay alive
I've used my deaths with greed and tenderness and will
with comfort happiness and praise
my grandiose stupidity
I want to live to live to live
please go away"
So cat jumped from the house to lawn
"I like it here I am I am," she said and leapt again
"Then listen or your time is through"
the apparition said
"your life is up to you; your comfort too
but learn to lean or dark will come again
lean or you will lose what light is left in you"

"Lean," said the cat

"obscene," said the cat

"if I lean I'm a worm if I lean I'm scum"

"If you don't, you're dumb," the apparition said

"No I won't and I can't I've no skill it's no good"

"It's that or this," the apparition said

and pointed to a hole, then fled

The cat stepped to then the cat stepped fro

then she arched her back

then she hunkered down low

"If I jump inside is that suicide?" she pondered

as the starry night neared

"There's low and there's low," she said to herself

Then she filled the hole with twigs and earth

"I've learned my lessons

I'm here to stay," she mewed with her head held high

Then off cat ran with a surety

that suggested new beauty and purity

rubbing briefly against a young oak tree

"It's a minor start but it's new to me," she said

which implied her sanity

and a rising *joie de vivre*.

ABOUT THE AUTHOR

Jan Freeman is the author of *Autumn Sequence* and *Hyena,* recipient of the Cleveland State University Poetry Center Award. Her poems have appeared in many journals and anthologies, including *The Oxford Companion to Women Writers in the United States, The Arc of Love, The American Poetry Review, The American Voice, The Massachusetts Review,* and *Chelsea.* She lives in western Massachusetts.

ABOUT PARIS PRESS

Paris Press is a young nonprofit press publishing the work of women writers who have been neglected or misrepresented by the literary world. Publishing one to two books a year, Paris Press values work that is daring in style and in its courage to speak truthfully about society, culture, history, and the human heart. To publish our books, Paris Press relies on generous support from organizations and individuals. Please help Paris Press keep the voices of essential women writers in print and known. All contributions are tax-deductible.

The type of this book is set in Sabon MT.
Cover design by Judythe Sieck.
Book design by Ivan Holmes.
Typesetting by R&S Book Composition.
Photograph of the author is by Carol Potter.